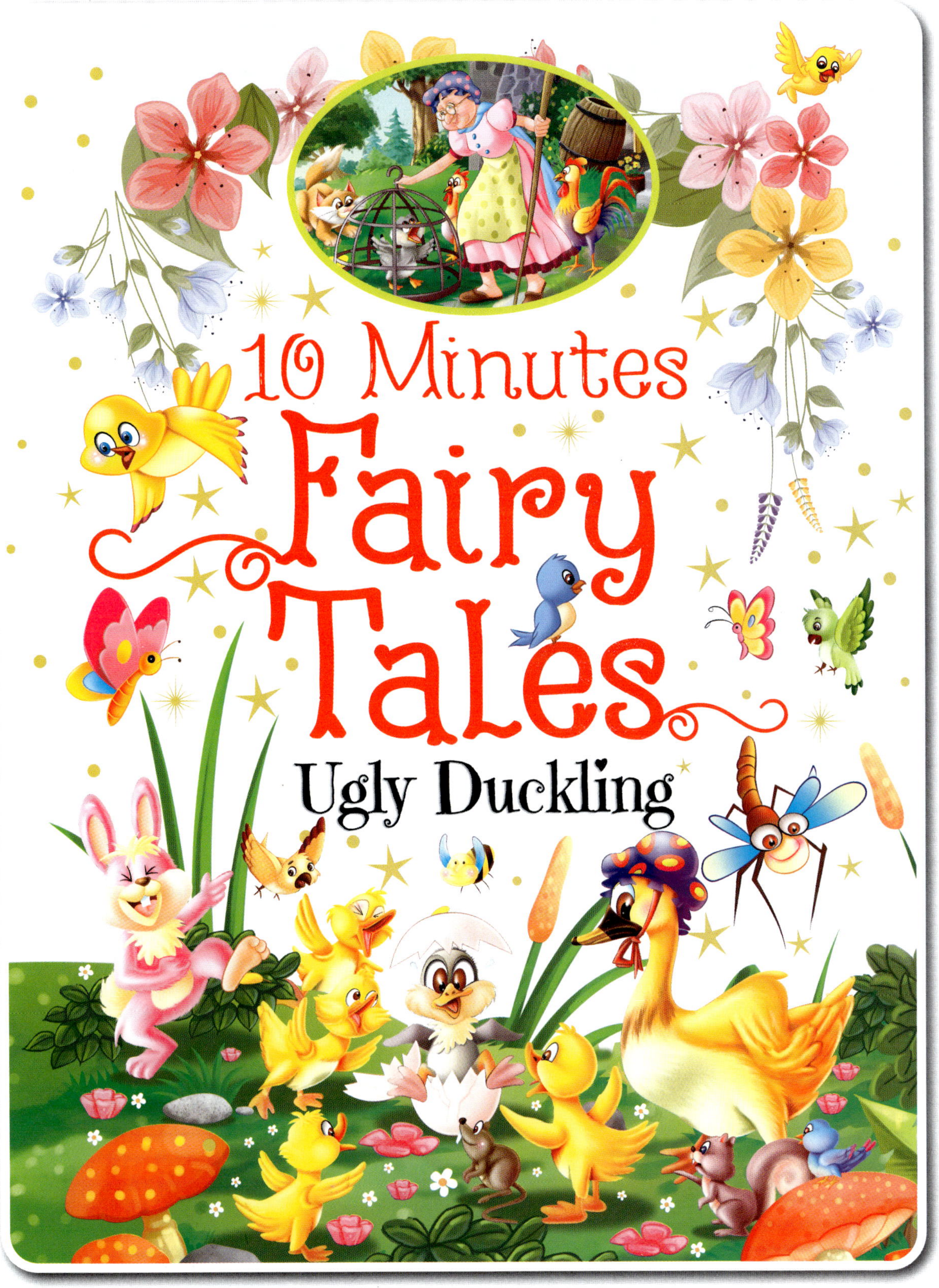
10 Minutes
Fairy Tales
Ugly Duckling

One day, the eggs of a duck started to hatch one by one. But when the seventh egg hatched, a young one crept forth, crying, "Peep, peep." He was very large and ugly! The mother duck wondered, "He looks different! His feathers are scruffy and he has large feet. But never mind, he will be kind at heart."

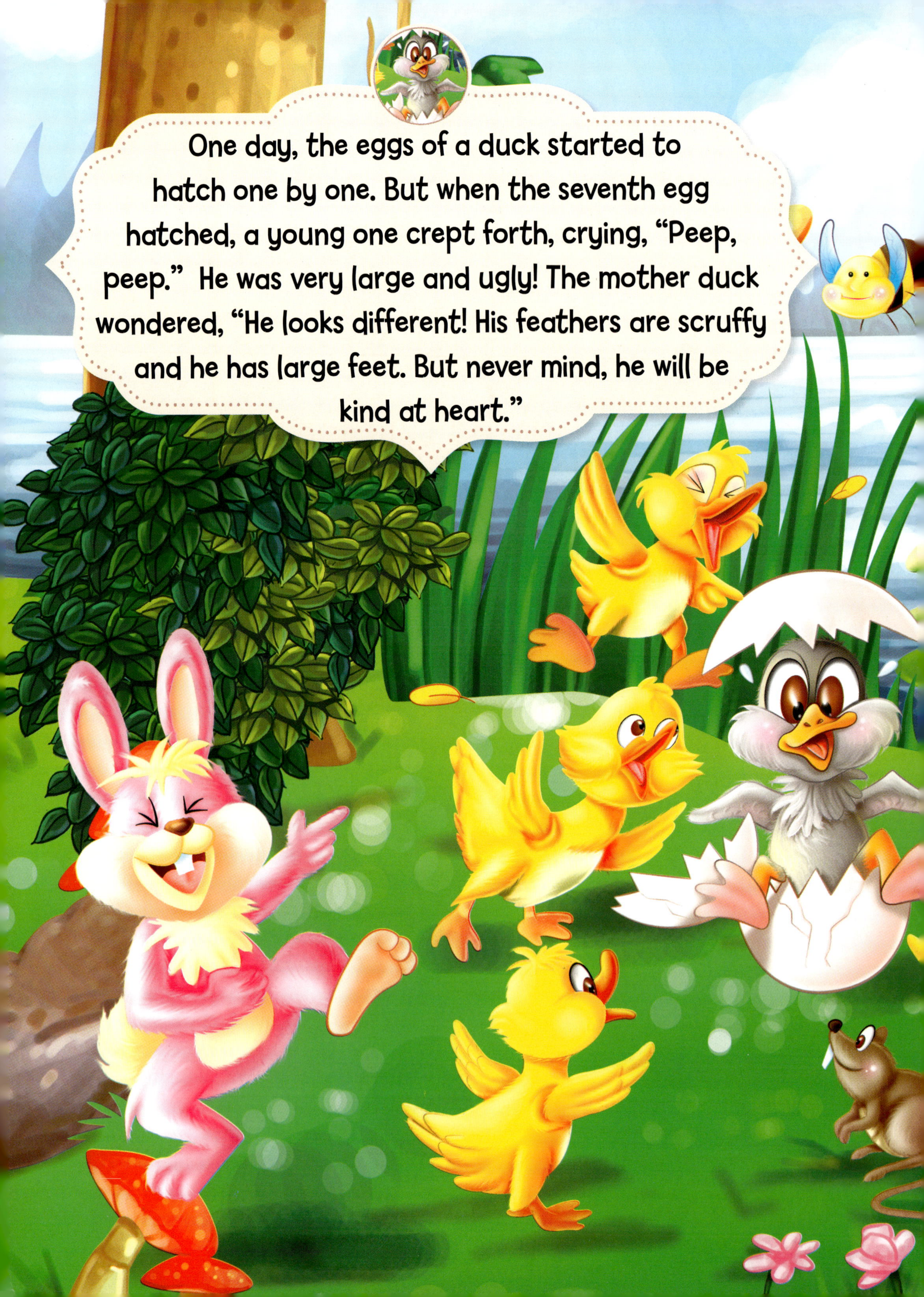

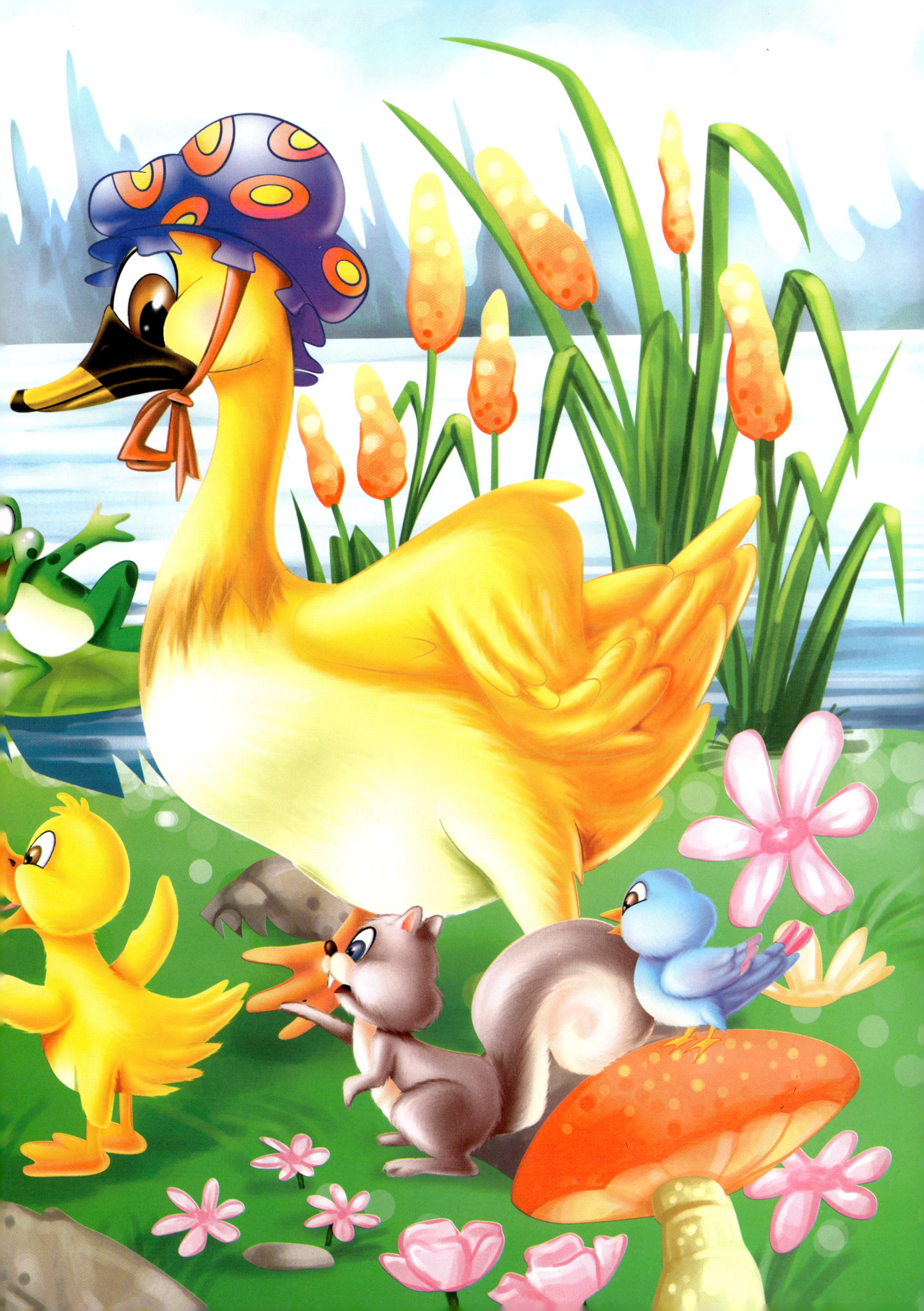

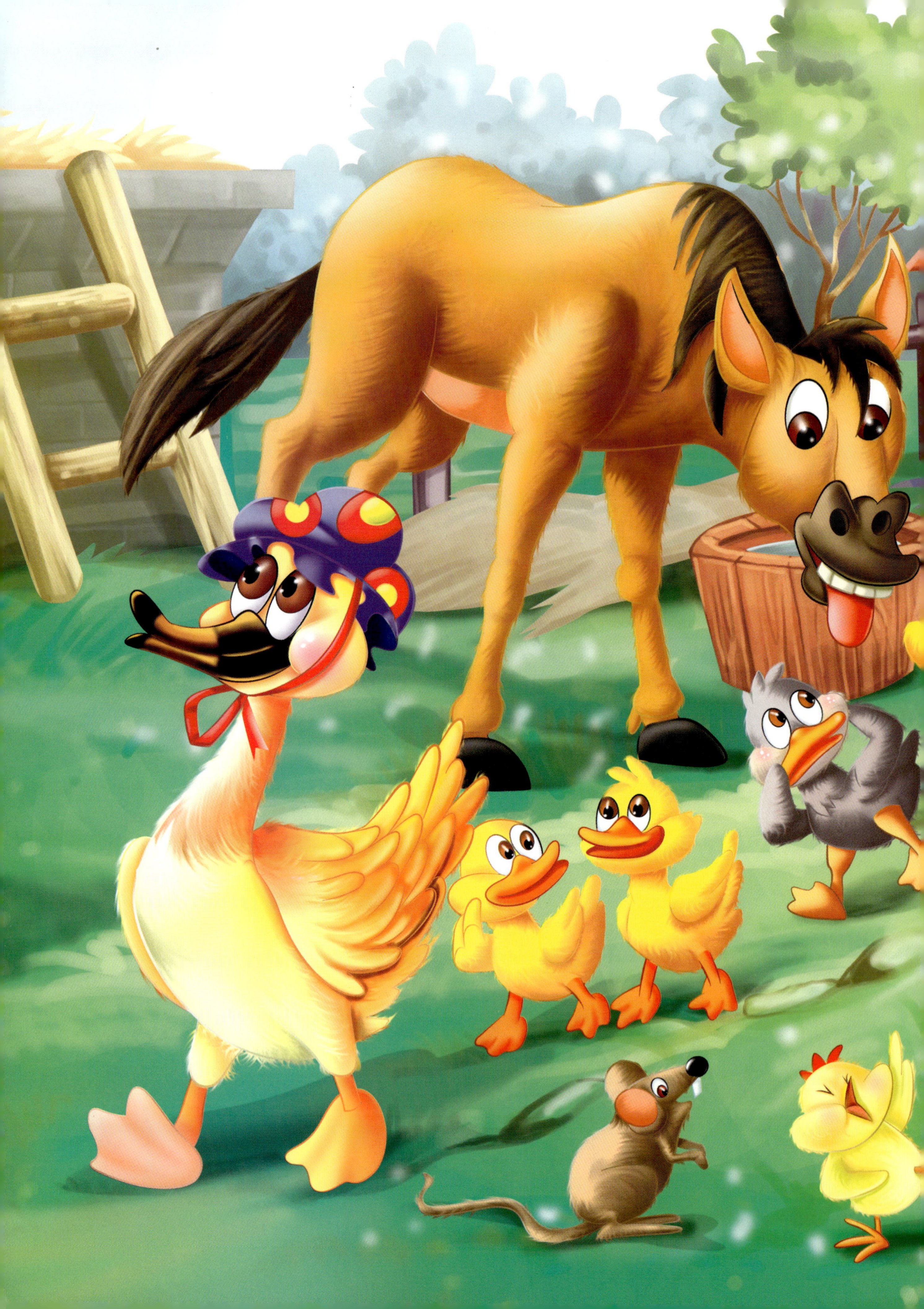

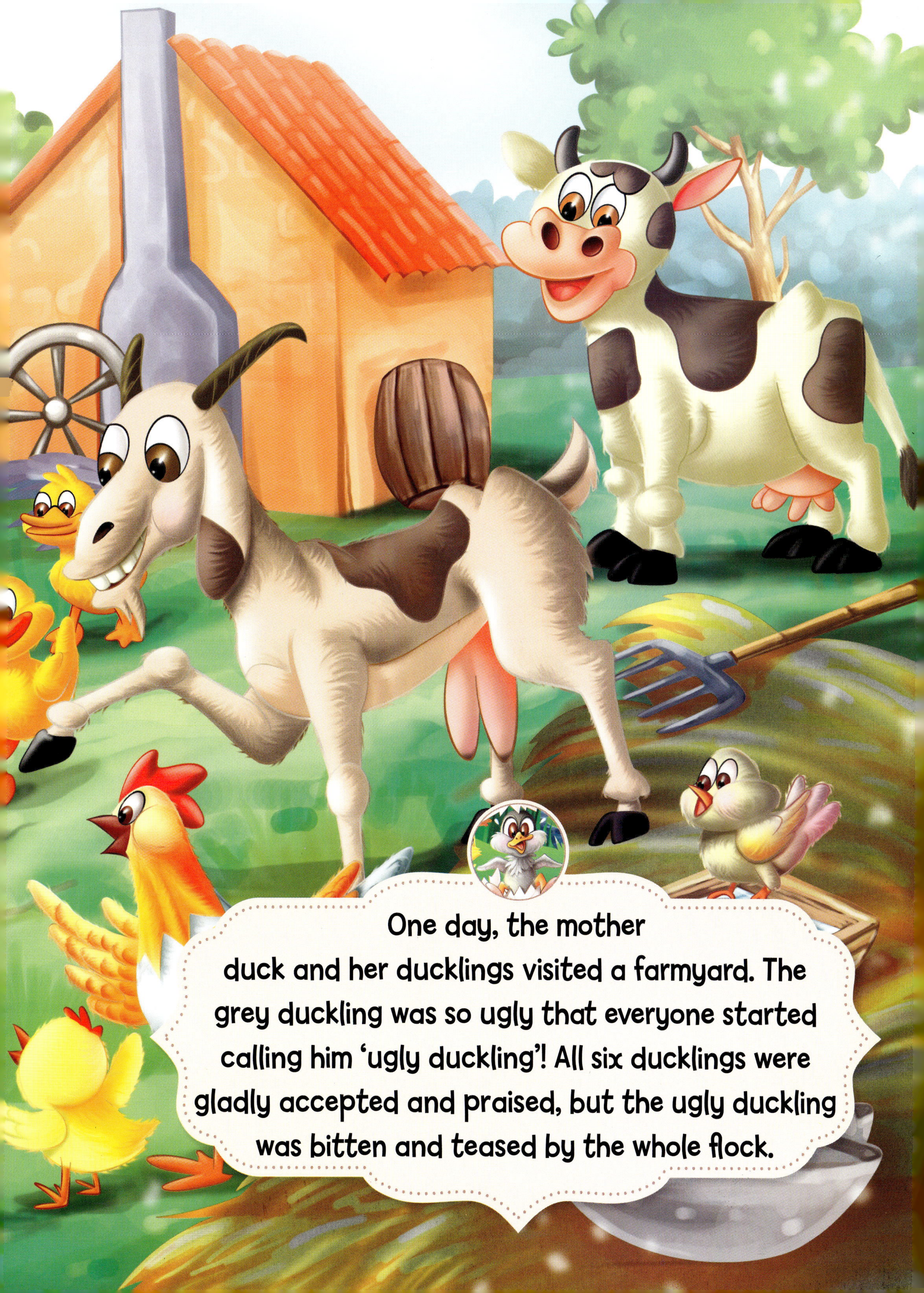

One day, the mother duck and her ducklings visited a farmyard. The grey duckling was so ugly that everyone started calling him 'ugly duckling'! All six ducklings were gladly accepted and praised, but the ugly duckling was bitten and teased by the whole flock.

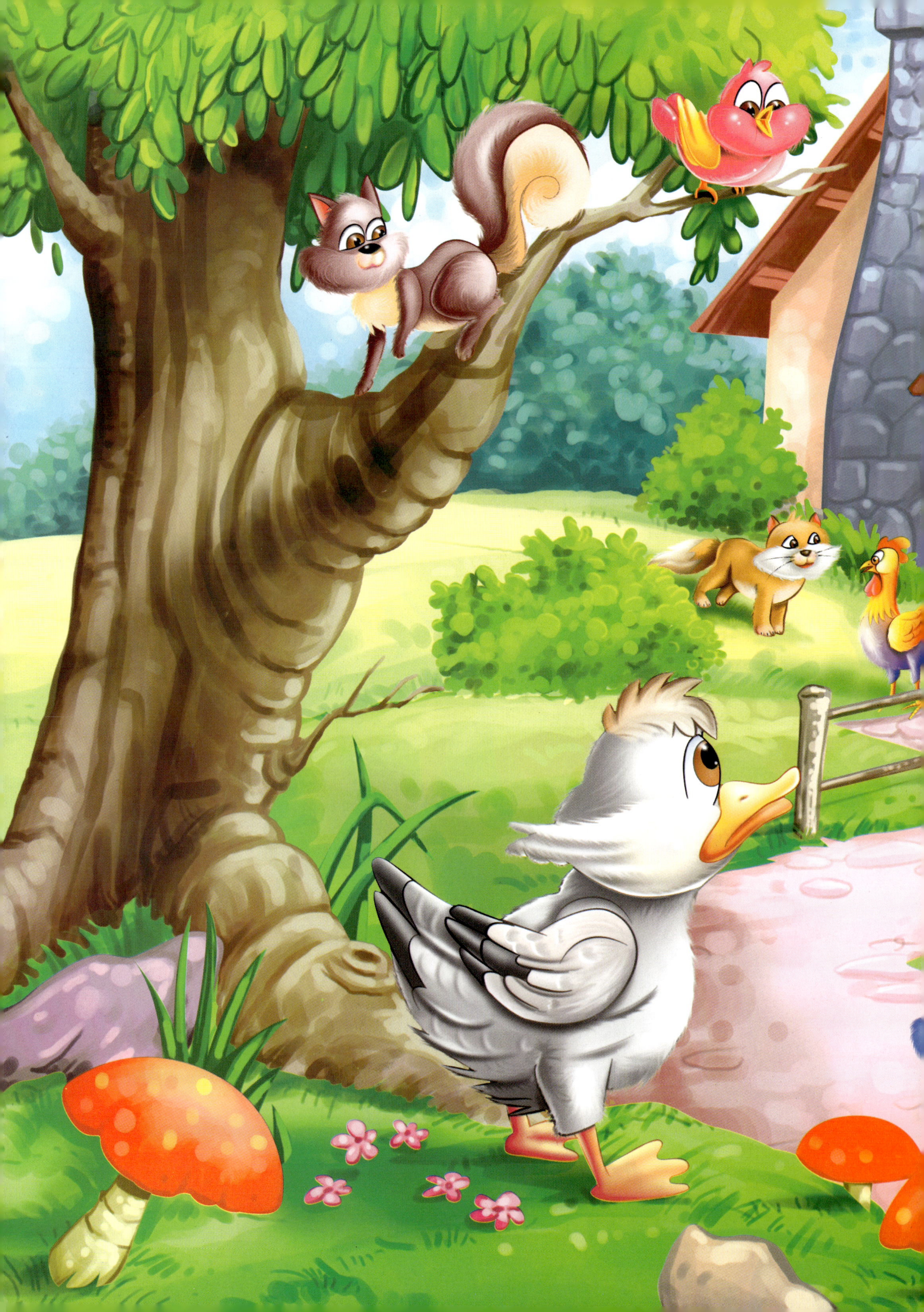

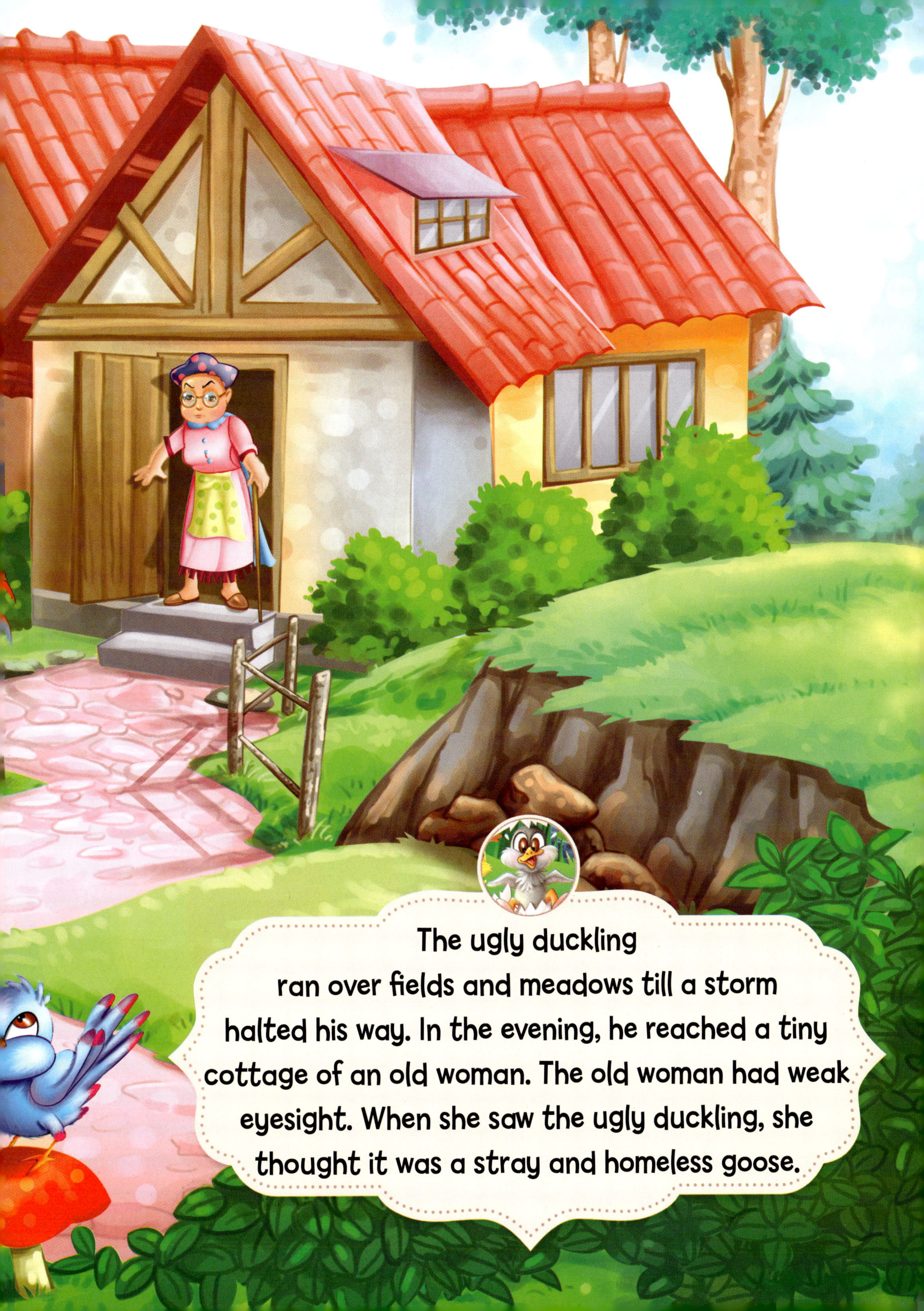

The ugly duckling
ran over fields and meadows till a storm
halted his way. In the evening, he reached a tiny
cottage of an old woman. The old woman had weak
eyesight. When she saw the ugly duckling, she
thought it was a stray and homeless goose.

But after a few days,
when he didn't lay eggs, the woman threw the ugly duckling out of the cottage. "Here you go. You are of no use to me," she shouted. Next, the duckling took shelter at the edge of a lake in the forest. It was winter, and the clouds, heavy with snowflakes, hung low in the sky.

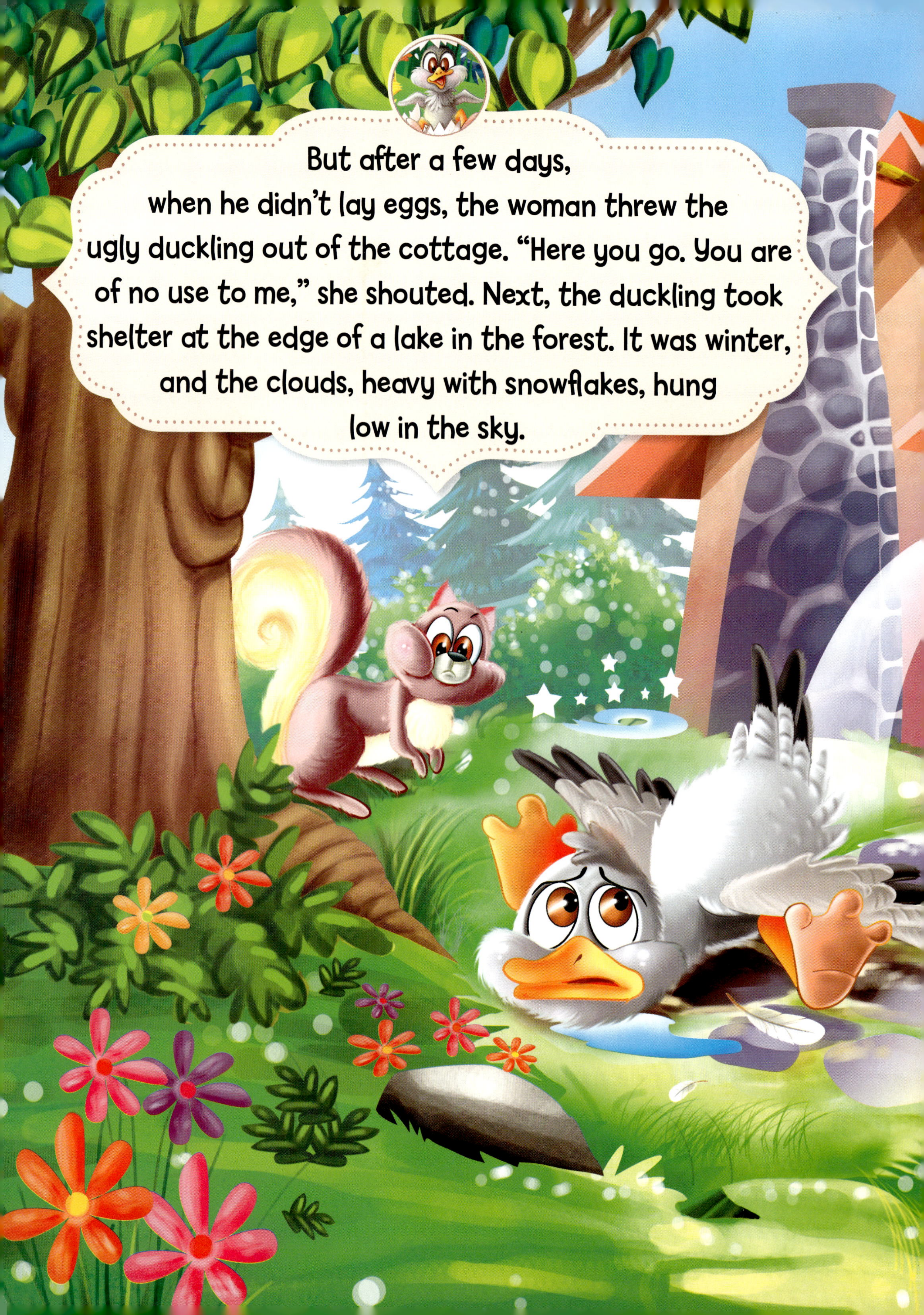

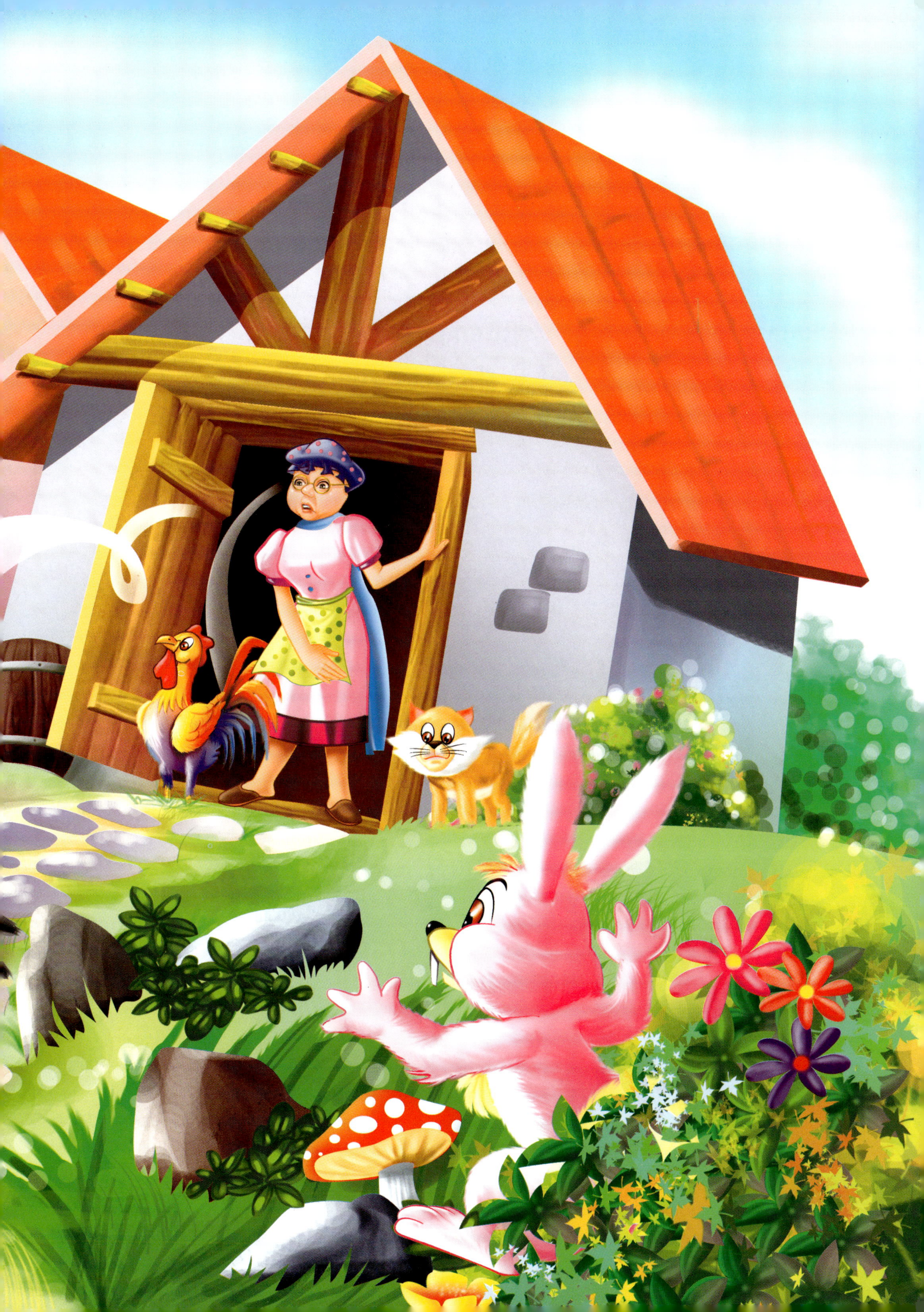

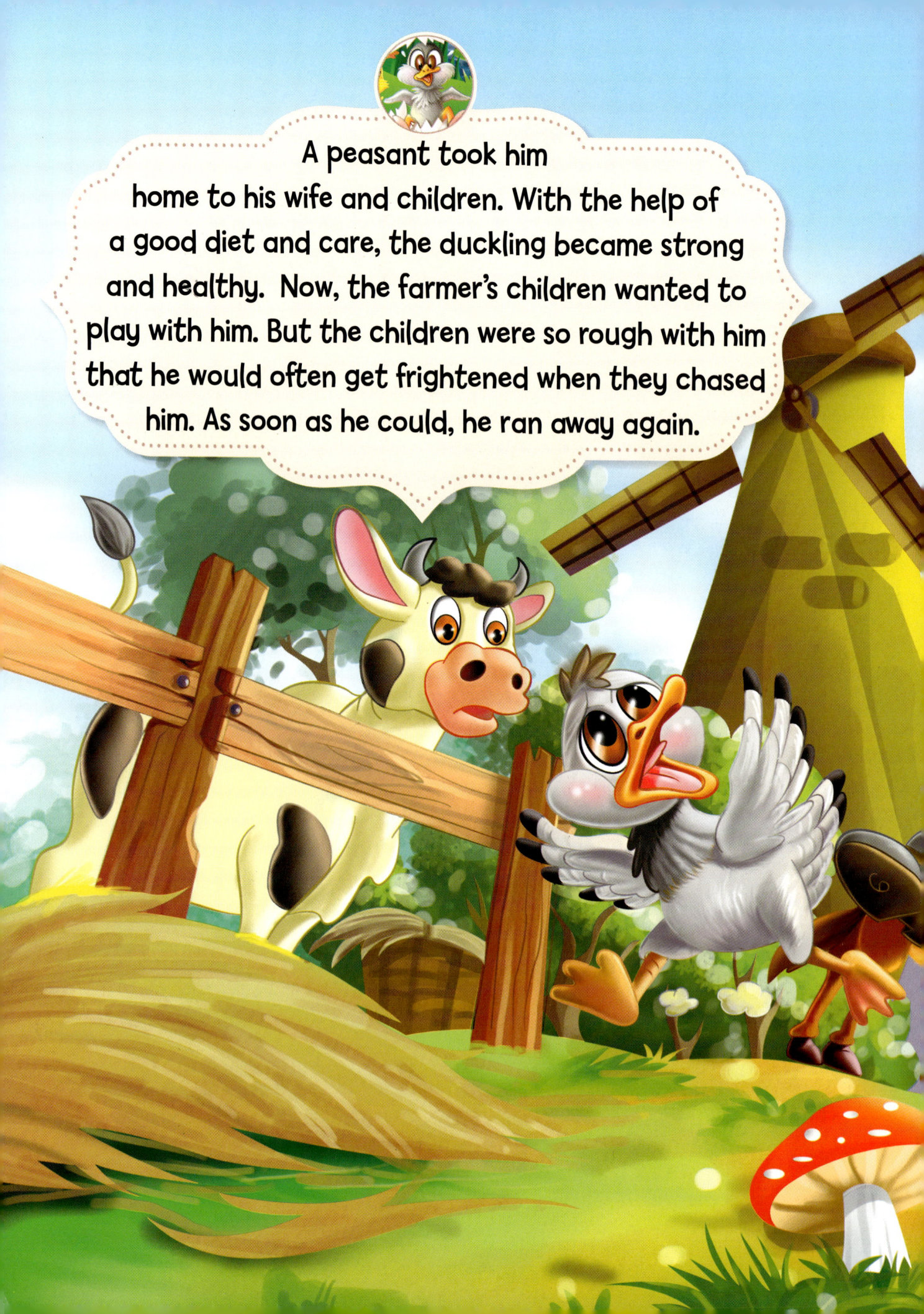

A peasant took him home to his wife and children. With the help of a good diet and care, the duckling became strong and healthy. Now, the farmer's children wanted to play with him. But the children were so rough with him that he would often get frightened when they chased him. As soon as he could, he ran away again.

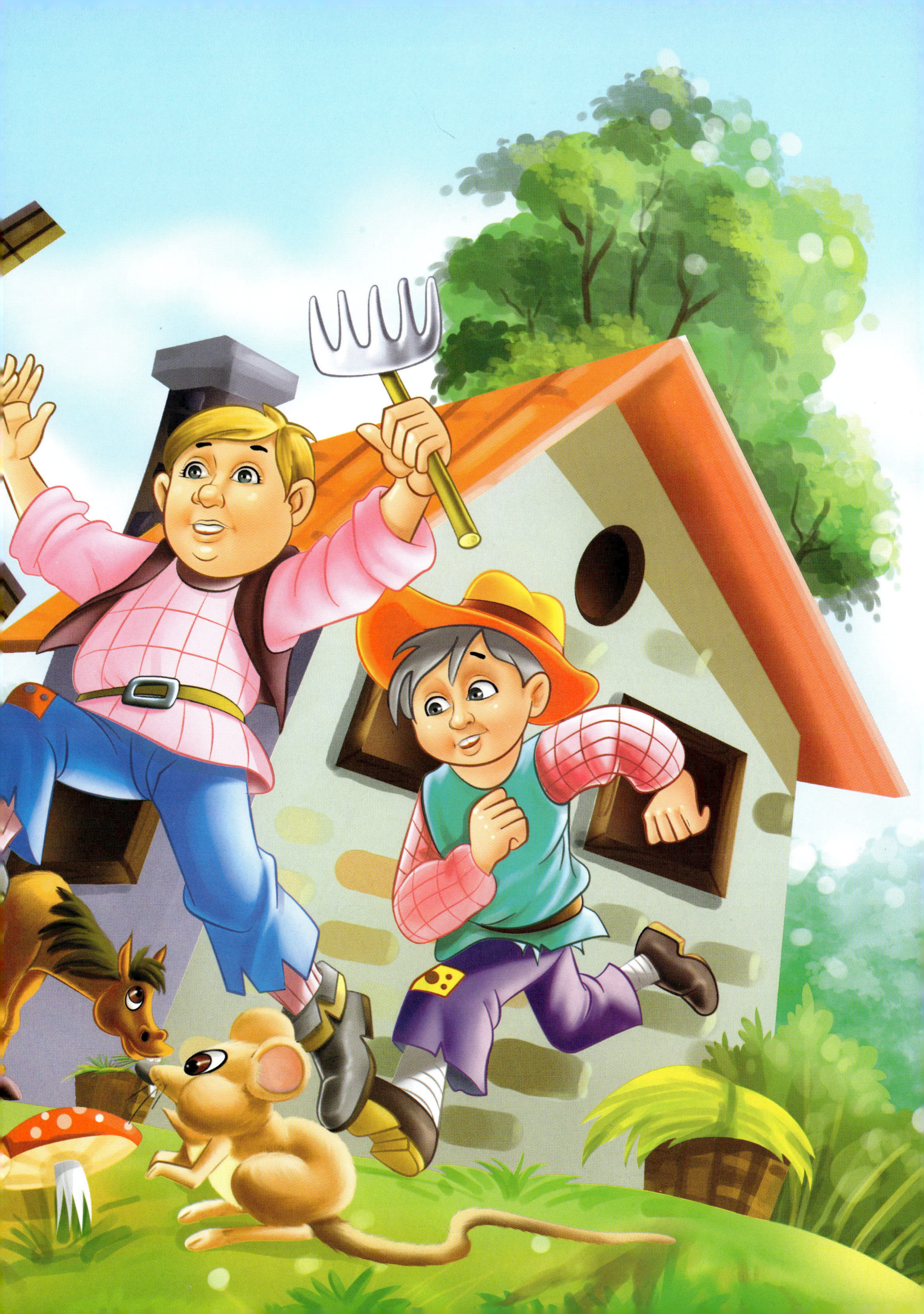

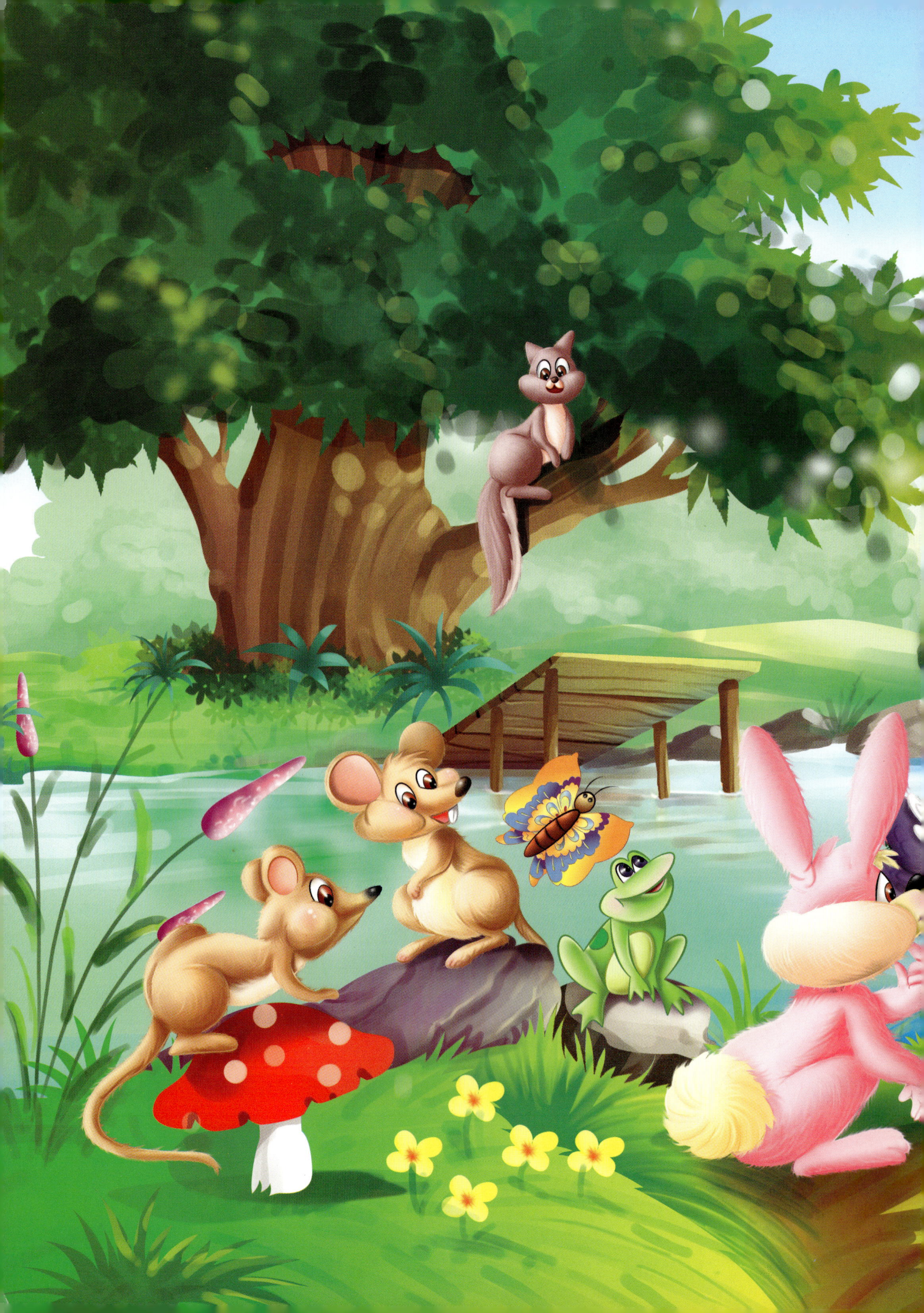

At last, the duckling found a safe hiding place among the reeds in the marsh. There he stayed for the rest of the winter. Then, after many long weeks, the warm spring sun began to shine again. The duckling spread his wings, which were strong now.

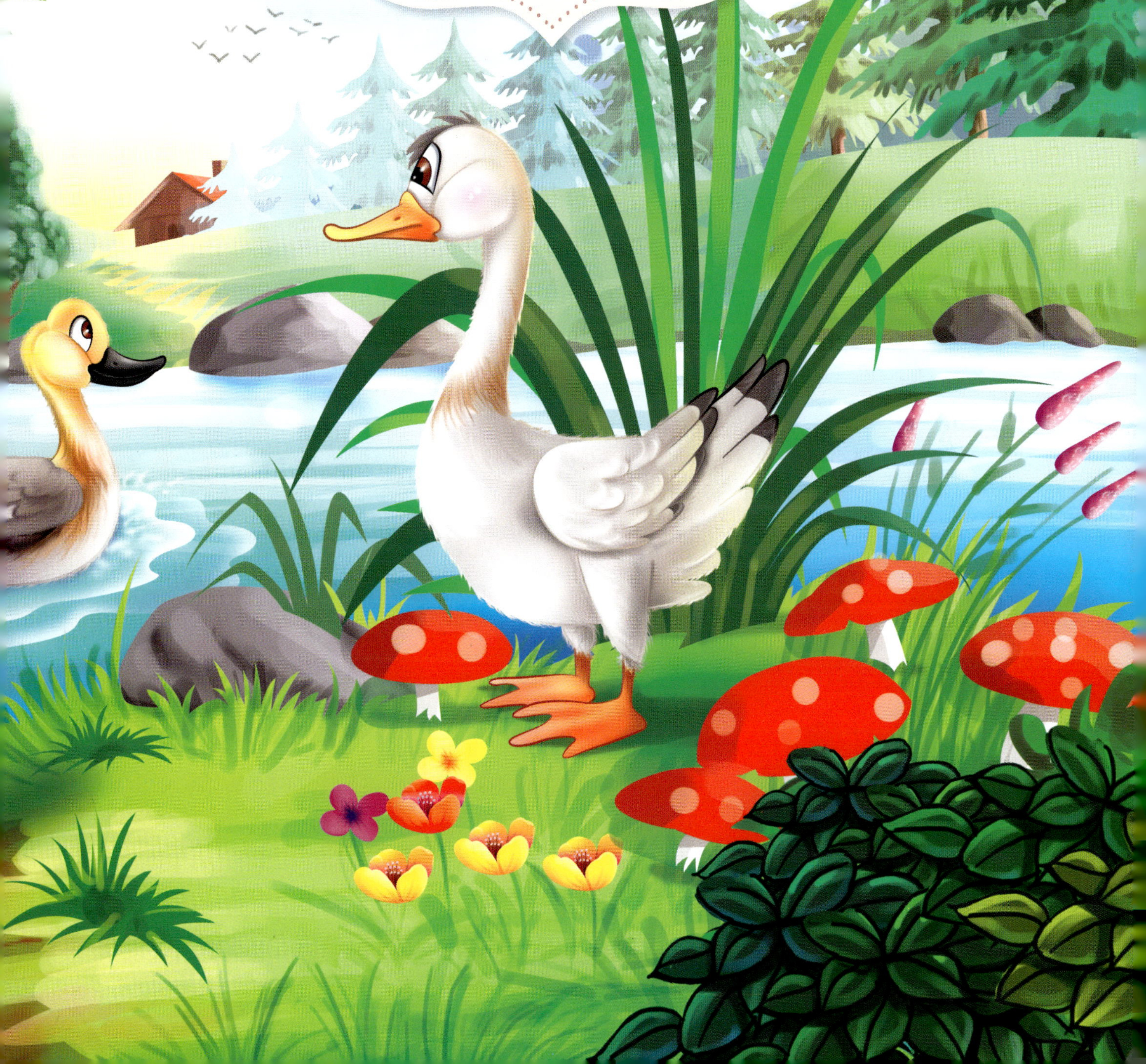

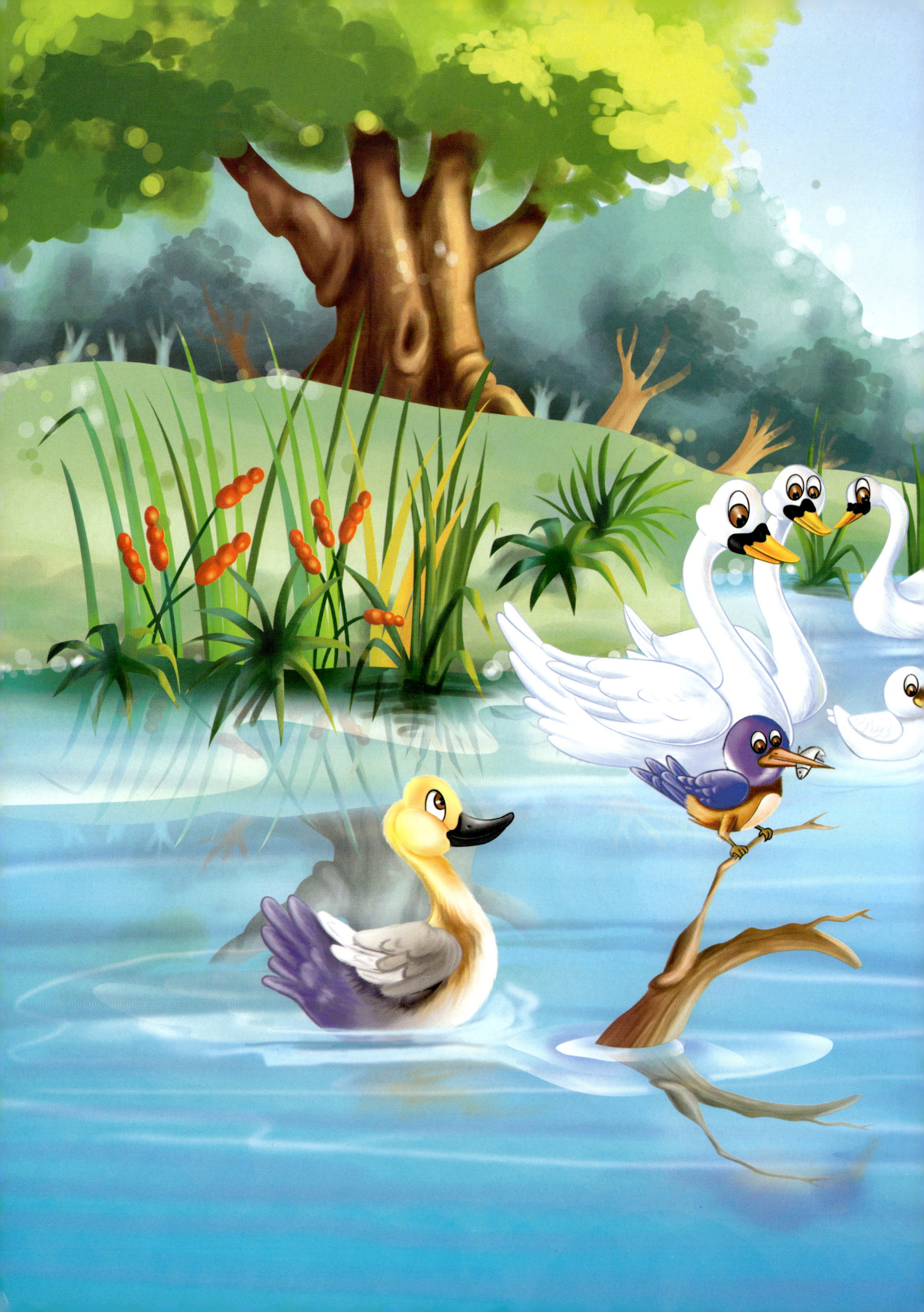

As he hung his head in grief, he saw his own reflection in the water. It was the image of a beautiful swan, not an ugly duckling! During the winter, he had grown into a beautiful white swan. The swans swam around the newcomer and stroked his neck with their beaks in welcome.

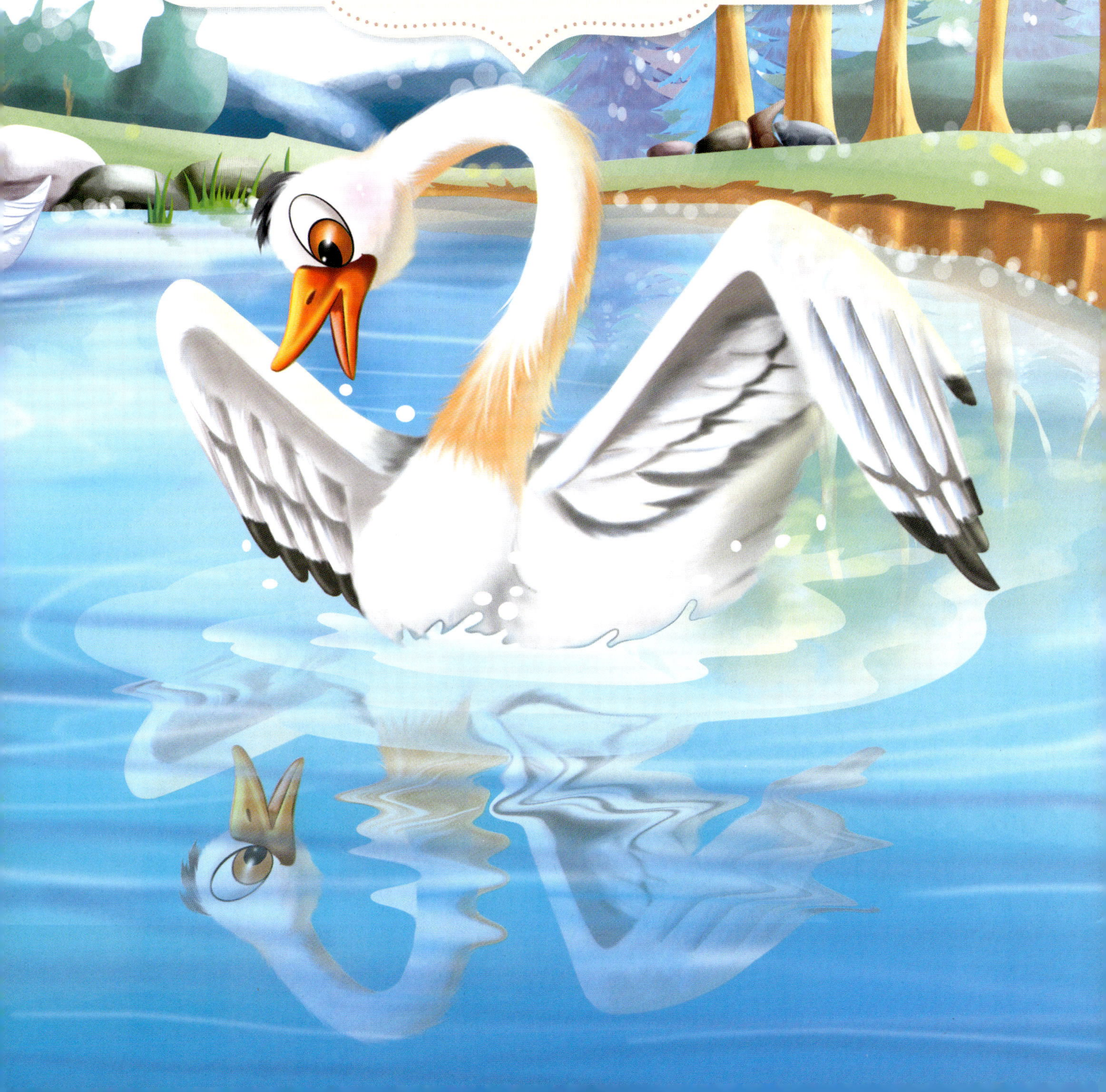

At last, the ugly duckling knew that he was a swan and not a duck. Thus, he was united with his true companions!